PULL IN CASE OF BOREDOM

Unforgettable cartoons!
At least to elephants!

by **Roy Schlemme**

First published by AuthorHouse 11/17/2011

ISBN: 978-1-4670-3920-8 (sc)
ISBN: 978-1-4670-3919-2 (ebk)

Library of Congress Control Number: 2011916927

This book is printed on acid-free paper.

Printed in the United States of America
Bloomington, Indiana

AuthorHouse™
1663 Liberty Drive
Bloomington, IN 47403
www.authorhouse.com
Phone: 1-800-839-8640

For Bernie and Amy
and Most everybody else.

A buggy gathering!

That title refers not only to our gang of goofy
entomologists seen above, but also to the following
126 pages of rollicking cartoons as well. Anybody seeking
respite from everyday problems, at least temporarily,
has come to the right place. However, rather than simply
taking the word of a certain money-grubbing cartoonist
who created them, do a test browse for yourself.
If not chuckling audibly within the first few moments,
it must be assumed there's something drastically wrong
with your funnybone. For all others, complete your perusal.
Uncontrollable laughter should subside within five
minutes of finishing. But enough of my idle chatter...
just fasten your seatbelts and enjoy!

—*Roy Schlemme*

"Always wondered how
this pub produced so many
first-rate darts players."

R. SCHLEMME

"Nice sideline, da Vinci...
but your contract calls for
Engines of War."

"Your *'Please allow exiting passengers to detrain.'*
was spot on, but I sensed a lack of assertive urgency
with *'Step in, you lifeless slugs! We'd all like to get home!'*."

"There was an eighth dwarf, Kinky...
but he ran off with a dominatrix."

"Sorry, it doesn't merit
a contract renegotiation."

"Hey, everybody, forget the siege.
They left their basement door open."

"A wise choice, sir. That per unit price
to you drops by over one-half on
our 96-pak of jute twine."

"Lose some wool...and fast!"

"So, which one better says,
'I'm more than a mere bystander
at this hate rally!'?"

"Believe it, kid! Your whole future depends on getting buried by some forgetful squirrel."

"Trust me."

R. SCHLEMME

R. SCHLEMME

"What you need to decide is whether this
is truly *'The Year of the Lapel'* or I'm
just screwing with your head to make a sale."

"You're charged with having been
'as high as an elephant's eye'."

"That's doable with a solid hit
on its Zimbabwe."

"...and when was your last encounter
with an accordion savant?"

How *Dutch Miniatures* compete.

R. SCHLEMME

"...and finally, very special wishes go out to our absent organist for a speedy recovery by next week."

"I suspect it's a glandular condition."

"You made a 'major consumer decision'
at the Snacks Counter. Now live with it!"

"Nothing personal, but I seldom socialize
outside my edibles sub-group."

"I'm thinkin' they just might
take the fort this time around."

"You're right, this tux does let me
see myself in a new light."

"So what do you do when you're not setting
autumn leaves aglow in brilliant golds and fiery scarlets?"

Oxymoron: Air passenger who, during
a flight emergency, decides to wear
his drop-down mask as a little party hat.

R. SCHLEMME

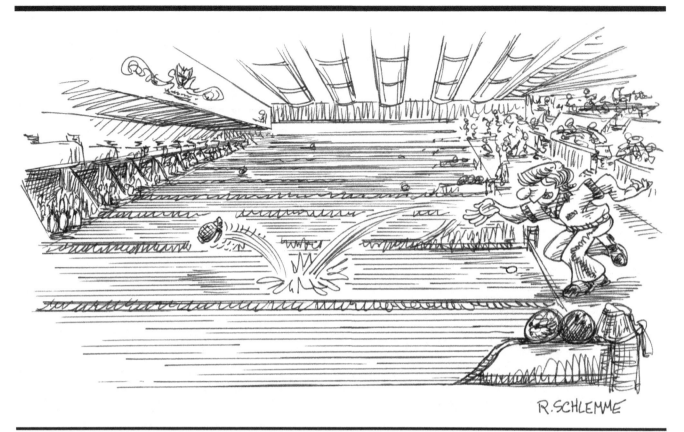

"Bark twice! I distinctly said, 'Bark twice
as soon as you spot our exit!'."

The Bermuda Tetrahedron

**Often blamed for the mysterious and
unexplained disappearances of
solid geometry instructors.**

R. SCHLEMME

"May we assume your outlying
guest cottages have AC?"

"It's just a little something I had thrown together
by a little something I had thrown together."

R. SCHLEMME

"Ah, Spring...when the sound of
achievement-obsessed parents fills the air."

MOTIVATION

WORKBOUND

HOMEBOUND

R. SCHLEMME

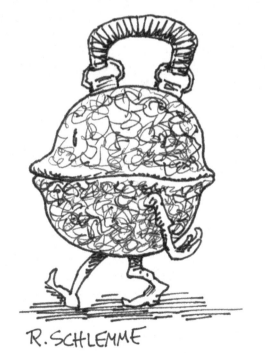

Walking nut case.
(...but with a handle on things.)

R. SCHLEMME

"Now that you've been approved,
it's time to work out a repayment schedule
with our loan specialist, Mr. Scar."

R. SCHLEMME

The Lady Who Didn't Know Beans.

"I feel a sneeze coming on!"

"You tango beautifully for a predator."

"So guys, let's talk a 'Hey, Diddle-diddle' follow-up."

"Just so you know, I tack on a surcharge
for woolly mammoth trims."

"Let's see...there's *Munch & Crunch, Lotsa Crunch, Bits o' Crunch, Grits n' Crunch, Crunch Bunches, Crunch Lumps, Clumps of Crunch, Muncha Buncha Crunch, Crock o' Crunch, Cracklin' Crunch...*"

"Well, so much for 'O great goddess Pelee,
how about putting a cork in it?'."

"Pâté, my ass! You're liverwurst!"

"Next time around. I'll bring along a few
Alpine Meadow strips to kill that nasty sulfur odor."

I CLAIM THIS DREARY LITTLE BISTRO IN THE NAME OF STARBUCKS FOR ALL THE WORLD'S CHRONICALLY PRETENTIOUS WASTRELS BENT ON DROPPING OBSCENE SUMS FOR CLEVERLY CHRISTENED COFFEES AS WELL AS AN ENDLESS ASSORTMENT OF ARTERY·CLOGGING CONFECTIONARY TIDBITS!!!

R·SCHLEMME

"The jokes can turn awfully mean
out here in the desert."

"Let's try it from the other end.
Do you see anything that doesn't
remind you of eucalyptus?"

R.SCHLEMME

"How come we never do show tunes?"

"To be honest, I still feel more
at home raiding and pillaging."

"Speak English! This is America!"

"Care for a sneak preview of my Spring Collection?"

"Sorry, we're *The Three Big Pigs.*
You want that single-story brick
across the street."

R. SCHLEMME

"Hi, Laura. As spokesbowl for your Tupperware,
I've been requested to question the quality of
muck you've been dumping into us lately."

"I've always admired architects able to
infuse their creations with wry humor."

R. SCHLEMME

"More *Food of the Gods*!"

"Think we might suspend troop
movements for evening mess, General?"

"...and now, to our final sticking point.
Who gets custody of the mirrors?"

Unstable launch rocket.

"It's very Dodge City."

"You've been bumped up to our short list.
We're running low on snotty-looking aristocrats."

"No hints, Mr. Carver, no hints."

"Hi. Mind if I react to a blatant display of
affluence by dumping my hot coffee on your head?"

NICHE MARKET GIFTWARE

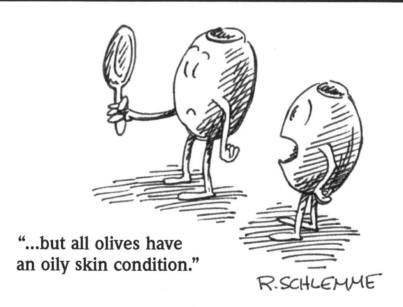

"...but all olives have
an oily skin condition."

"I've always depended on the kindness
of passing strangers in 18-wheelers."

"Ease off, Tim! You're home now!"

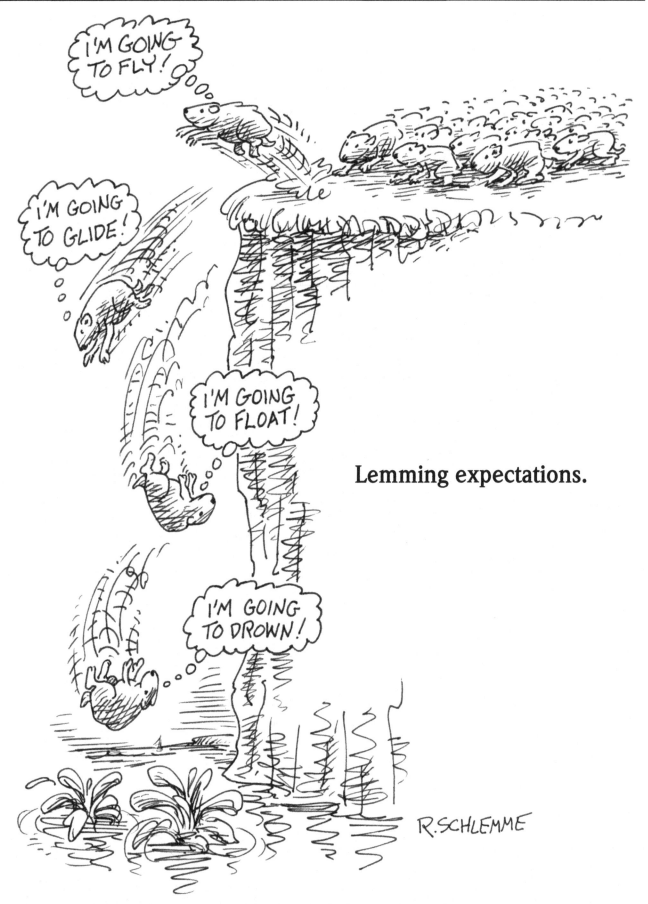

Lemming expectations.

R. SCHLEMME

"As to your specific event, Mister Jehosaphat, is that 'The Broad Jump' or 'The High Jump'?"

"You have the right to remain silent..."

"I'm genuinely surprised. Sending out
a nice fruitcake usually gets better results."

"It'll be hard, but disregard
any spectators yelling *'Roll over!'*."

"Pilobolus is here for their appointment."

"Rumor has it that, at some future point,
they'll be smaller, cuter and
covered with nice, fluffy feathers."

R. SCHLEMME

"Always shut the door when you leave!
Always shut the door when you leave!"

Line art specialist.

"Future CEOs don't bunt ."

R. SCHLEMME

"Mona Timmerman,
this is your future speaking!"

R. SCHLEMME

"Sure, I know the wish was made
when you were six. I had a backlog."

"Without you, I'm nothing."

R. SCHLEMME

"...and what did we discuss about getting into entanglements with strangers?"

R. SCHLEMME

"Today, gentlemen, I propose that we try to
land a fish first, before resuming our
discussion on quantum theory."

"You should know, this'll be
my first love handles exorcism."

R. SCHLEMME

"Now that, people, is a
more marketable tag."

"Stay very still! Mitzi's bonding!"

"Nothing against running a little
second business on the side."

"Don't deny it; I saw the bubbles!
You just did a butt trumpet solo!"

"Lloyd, deep fly left sideline,
then sprint out through Gate C
and keep going. You've been cut."

R.SCHLEMME

R.SCHLEMME

Glutton's fate at
an 'All-you-can-eat'
pancake breakfast.

"So what do you suppose might
lure him out of <u>his</u> hole?"

R. SCHLEMME

"Don't swerve or we'll never earn their respect!"

"Since you all qualify for the job, we'll decide
with Elevator Bingo. First applicant correctly
predicting *'A floor lit four across'* gets hired."

"I suppose no one
questioned why he would
order twenty 'Big Whoppers'
for his last meal?"

"They're extremely bright, clean, friendly and delicious with scrambled eggs."

R. SCHLEMME

FOR THE FULL STORY
LOG ON TO:
GUTTEDSOUL.COM

R. SCHLEMME

"So that's how people get
instilled with the fear of God."

"Hey, guys...can you tell me
if I'm still on the road to extinction?"

R. SCHLEMME

"Tidying before festooning, Carl!
Tidying before festooning!"

R. SCHLEMME

R. SCHLEMME

"It's actually rather common in
patients who come from Alabama."

The Closest Crosstown Bus Stop

(A BALLETIC HAIKU MOMENT)

SIXTH AVENUE IS WHERE
WE SHOULD HEAD.
BROADWAY LIES
MUCH TOO FAR AWAY.

R. SCHLEMME

"Hollywood might be wise
to read this as an omen."

"Don't worry, son. The bad ones
introduce themselves pretty quickly."

"You're right, it doesn't work.
Try that glass of champagne
in place of the torch."

R. SCHLEMME

"Ernie, you were made
for the trumpet."

"Whenever I'm feeling a little down, I just tell myself–
'*Hey, you're one of the building blocks of life!*'."

"Your genetics experiments are
beginning to frighten me a bit, Jim."

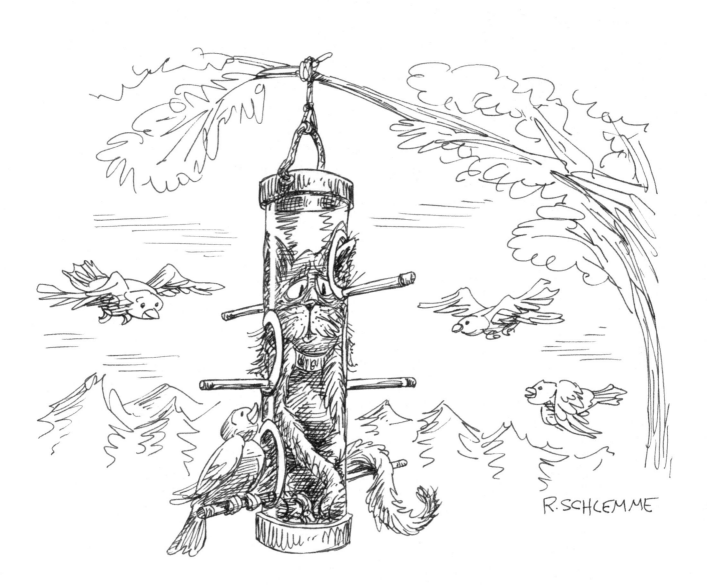

R.SCHLEMME

"So, professor, when did you and your fun-loving associates at The National Weather Center conclude that replacing the extreme thunderstorm alert with a snippet of *hot phone sex* might constitute a sophomoric prank gone awry?"

"Brigette doesn't speak, but she occasionally
jots down brief inspirational poems."

"I see your problems as more metal than physical."

"All I got told was that our seats were field-level."

"Thought you'd like to know that we all find you a great inspiration."

R. SCHLEMME

"Why can't you just buckle and heave
quietly like the rest of us?"

"Stump glue!"

"Still a touch off the mark."

"I came! I saw! I conked out!"

"My first interview question is:
How did you make it through
that doorway with those antlers?"

It ain't over till it's over!

In the event you've enjoyed Roy Schlemme's
cartoon takes in *Pull In Case Of Boredom*,
and seek a little encore, then by all means,
contact **authorhouse.com** immediately
to order one or more of his like-minded
previously published offerings:
*Skewed Views, Skewed Views Too,
The Moon's First Banana*
and/or *Lightin' Up.*